HEINEMANN GUIDED READERS

ELEMENTARY LEVEL

SIR ARTHUR CONAN DOYLE
The Lost World

Retold by Anne Collins

HEINEMANN

HEINEMANN GUIDED READERS
ELEMENTARY LEVEL

Series Editor: John Milne

The Heinemann Guided Readers provide a choice of enjoyable reading material for learners of English. The series is published at five levels – Starter, Beginner, Elementary, Intermediate and Upper. At **Elementary Level**, the control of content and language has the following main features:

Information Control

Stories have straightforward plots and a restricted number of main characters. Information which is vital to the understanding of the story is clearly presented and repeated when necessary. Difficult allusion and metaphor are avoided and cultural backgrounds are made explicit.

Structure Control

Students will meet those grammatical features which they have already been taught in their elementary course of studies. Other grammatical features occasionally occur with which the students may not be so familiar, but their use is made clear through context and reinforcement. This ensures that the reading as well as being enjoyable provides a continual learning situation for the students. Sentences are kept short – a maximum of two clauses in nearly all cases – and within sentences there is a balanced use of simple adverbial and adjectival phrases. Great care is taken with pronoun reference.

Vocabulary Control

At **Elementary Level** there is a limited use of a carefully controlled vocabulary of approximately 1,100 basic words. At the same time, students are given some opportunity to meet new or unfamiliar words in contexts where their meaning is obvious. The meaning of words introduced in this way is reinforced by repetition. Help is also given to the students in the form of vivid illustrations which are closely related to the text.

Contents

    A Note About the Author   4
    A Note About the Story   5
    The People in This Story   6

1 I Meet Professor Challenger   8
2 The Professor's Story   13
3 Our Journey Begins   17
4 The River Amazon   21
5 A Terrible Thing Happens   25
6 Creatures From the Past   30
7 Death in the Night   35
8 A Dreadful Walk   40
9 Prisoners of the Ape-People   44
10 The Battle   49
11 Escape From the Lost World   53
12 We Return to London   57

    Points for Understanding   61

A Note About the Author

Arthur Conan Doyle was born in Edinburgh, Scotland on 22nd May, 1859. He studied medicine at Edinburgh University and he became a doctor in 1881. However, Conan Doyle did not earn much money as a doctor. So he started writing books, plays and articles.

He liked writing historical stories and adventure stories. But in 1887, Conan Doyle wrote a detective story – *A Study in Scarlet*. This story made Conan Doyle famous. The story was about a brilliant detective, Sherlock Holmes, and his assistant, Dr Watson. The Sherlock Holmes stories are: *The Adventures of Sherlock Holmes*, *The Case-Book of Sherlock Holmes*, *The Memoirs of Sherlock Holmes*, *The Return of Sherlock Holmes*, *His Last Bow*, *A Study in Scarlet*, *The Sign of Four*, *The Hound of the Baskervilles* and *The Valley of Fear*.

In 1893, Conan Doyle wrote the story, *The Final Problem*. Sherlock Holmes dies in this story. But readers did not like it. They were angry and upset that Holmes was dead. They wrote hundreds of letters to Conan Doyle. At last, Conan Doyle wrote another story about Sherlock Holmes. Holmes comes back to life in *The Empty House*.

Conan Doyle did many interesting things in his life. When he was a young man he worked on a ship. In 1900, he went to South Africa. He worked in a hospital there during the Boer War. He travelled to America, Australia, Africa and Europe. In these countries he talked about his books, politics and social problems. He also became a detective! He found evidence to help prisoners who were not guilty. They were later set free.

Conan Doyle was married twice. In 1885, he married Louise Hawkins. They were married for 21 years and had two children. Louise died in 1906. Conan Doyle married his second wife, Jean Leckie, in 1907. They had three children. Conan Doyle and Jean were married for 23 years. Arthur Conan Doyle was given a knighthood in 1902. Sir Arthur Conan Doyle died on 7th July, 1930. He was 71 years old.

A Note About the Story

The Lost World was written in 1912. This is an exciting and unusual adventure story. Sir Arthur Conan Doyle writes about a land where creatures from the past still live.

For many hundreds of years, scientists have thought about how life began on Earth. Since about 400 BC people have found the bones of enormous animals in the ground. At first, no one knew which animals the bones came from.

Today, we know more about these creatures. We know that they lived between 245 and 64 MILLION years ago. They were the largest creatures that ever lived.

In this story you will read about creatures with strange names. This list will help you:

stegosaurus	steg-o-sorus
pterodactyl	terr-o-daktil
iguanodon	ig-u-wano-don
allosaurus	all-o-sorus
megalosaurus	meg-all-o-sorus
tyrannosaurus rex	ti-rann-o-sorus reks

The People in This Story

Professor George Challenger
a zoologist. A scientist who studies animals

Edward Malone
a reporter on the *Daily Gazette* newspaper

Mr McArdle
the Editor of the *Daily Gazette*. Ed Malone's boss

Professor Summerlee
a scientist

Lord John Roxton
a traveller

The Ape-King
the leader of the Ape-People

The Prince
of the Indians

Sancho
a servant

Miguel
a servant

Gomez
a servant

1
I Meet Professor Challenger

My name is Edward Malone. I have a very strange and wonderful story to tell. Perhaps people will not believe my story. But everything in my story is true.

In 1912, I was twenty-three years old. I was working as a reporter for a newspaper in London. My job was to find out about things that had happened. Then I wrote about them in the newspaper. The name of the newspaper was the *Daily Gazette*.

My boss at the *Daily Gazette* was called Mr McArdle. Mr McArdle had worked for the newspaper for many years. He sent me to find news stories. I liked Mr McArdle and he liked me. I worked hard and enjoyed my job.

One morning, Mr McArdle called me into his office. He was reading one of my news reports.

'Congratulations, Malone,' said Mr McArdle. 'You are doing some very good work. You are a very good reporter. Are you happy in your job?'

'Yes, of course,' I said. I was pleased that Mr McArdle liked my work. Then I said, 'But I want to ask you something.'

'What is it?' said Mr McArdle.

'Well,' I said, 'I was thinking ... Please, Mr McArdle, could you send me on an adventure?'

'An adventure!' said Mr McArdle. 'What do you mean?'

'I'm a young man,' I said, 'and I want to do something exciting. Something exciting and dangerous. Then I can write about it for the *Daily Gazette*.'

'I see,' said Mr McArdle. He thought. Then he said, 'Have you heard of Professor Challenger?'

'Professor Challenger?' I said in surprise. 'Do you mean the famous scientist? Yes, I've heard of him. But I don't know much about him.'

'Professor Challenger is a zoologist,' said Mr McArdle. 'He studies the lives and the behaviour of animals. He is an expert in his work. He is very clever and knows many things.

'Two years ago, Professor Challenger went to South America alone. He stayed there for several months. When he came back, he said some very interesting things.'

'What kind of things?' I asked.

'He said he found some wonderful animals in South America. These animals were very large and unusual. Nobody had ever seen them before.

'But many people don't believe Professor Challenger. They think he is lying about the animals. Go and interview Challenger. Talk to him. Find out if he is telling the truth.'

'All right,' I said. Then I remembered something I had heard about Professor Challenger.

'Wait a minute,' I said. 'Professor Challenger hates reporters, doesn't he? He hit one reporter on the head. Then he threw another one down the stairs.'

'Yes,' said Mr McArdle. 'So if you want to interview him, you must be clever. That's all now, Malone. I have a lot of work to do. Goodbye!'

After I left Mr McArdle's office, I thought for a long time.

'Professor Challenger is very clever,' I thought, 'but he's also bad-tempered. He hates reporters. So he must not find out that I'm a reporter.'

I went to a library where old newspapers were kept. There were many articles about Professor Challenger in these newspapers. One article was about a talk he gave in Vienna.

I read the article. Then I had an idea. I decided to write a letter to Professor Challenger. The letter said:

> Dear Professor Challenger
>
> I am a student of science. I read about the talk you gave in Vienna. Your ideas are very interesting. But I do not understand all of them. Please can I visit you to talk about your ideas? Can I come on Wednesday morning at 11 o'clock?
>
> Yours sincerely
> *Edward D. Malone*

Two days later, I received a reply. It said:

> Dear Mr Malone
>
> Thank you for your letter. I am sorry you did not understand my ideas. They were very clear. Only a stupid person could not understand. However, if you want to see me, come to my house on Wednesday.
>
> Yours sincerely
> *George Challenger*

On Wednesday morning, I went to Professor Challenger's house. A servant showed me into the Professor's room.

The Professor was sitting at his desk. The desk was covered with books, maps and drawings. I stared at the Professor in surprise.

Professor Challenger had an enormous head. It was the largest head I had ever seen. He had a red face, grey eyes and a long black beard. His hands were big and strong and covered with thick black hair.

'Who are you?' he said rudely. 'What do you want?'

'Good morning, Professor,' I said. 'I'm Edward Malone, the science student. You sent me a letter. You asked me to come and see you this morning.'

'Oh yes,' said the Professor. 'Well, what don't you understand about my work?'

I asked the Professor some questions about his ideas. But it was very difficult. My questions were not very good. I did not know anything about science. The Professor listened.

After a few minutes he said, 'Shall I tell you something, Mr Malone?'

'Oh yes, Professor Challenger, please do.'

The Professor jumped up from his chair and came towards me. I was surprised. He was very short.

'Mr Malone, you are not a science student. Your questions are very stupid. You don't know anything about science. Shall I tell you what I think? I think you are a reporter!'

'Please, Professor—' I said. I was very worried. I moved away but the Professor followed me.

'I'm going to throw you out of my house,' he said. 'I threw out all the other reporters too!'

He ran towards me and pushed me through the door into the hall. The Professor held me around the neck and we fell to the floor. We rolled together across the hall. The servant opened the front door and we went out into the street.

'What's going on here?' asked a voice.

It was a policeman. He was standing beside us.

'Why are you fighting? Has this man hurt you?' the policeman asked me.

I did not want the Professor to be in trouble.

'No, no,' I said. 'It was my fault. I did something wrong.'

'Stop fighting, then,' said the policeman and he walked away.

Professor Challenger looked at me. He was smiling.

'Good,' he said. 'Now come back inside the house. I have something very interesting to show you.'

'Mr Malone, you are not a science student.
I think you are a reporter!'

I was still worried by the Professor. But I followed him inside. The servant closed the door.

2

The Professor's Story

Professor Challenger took me back to his room.

I had told the policeman everything was my fault. So the Professor was very pleased with me. He began to like me. He decided to tell me things.

'Sit down, Mr Malone,' he said. 'I'm going to talk to you about my journey to South America. But first you must promise me something.'

'What's that?' I asked.

'Don't put my story in your newspaper,' said the Professor. 'Do you understand?'

'All right,' I said.

'Good,' said the Professor. 'Listen. Two years ago I went on a journey to South America. I wanted to explore the forest round the River Amazon. I'm a zoologist. I wanted to find out about the animals there.

'We don't know very much about the Amazon forest. Not many Europeans have ever been there. The forest is very thick and dark. Many strange creatures live there – animals, birds and insects. Some of them are very dangerous.

'But some people live in the Amazon forest too. These people are Indians. One day I came to a small Indian village. The Indians had found a stranger in the forest. They had brought him to their village. But he was very ill.'

'Was he an Indian?' I asked.

'No,' said Professor Challenger. 'He was an American. But when I saw him, he was dead.

'The man's bag was beside him. I looked inside the bag and found his name and address. His name was Maple White. His home was in Michigan, in America.

'There was also a box of paints and some paintbrushes in the bag. So I knew that the dead American had been an artist. I found something in the pocket of his jacket. It was a book of drawings.'

Professor Challenger opened a drawer in his desk. He took out a notebook. The cover of the book was old and dirty.

'This is Maple White's book of drawings,' he said.

I took the notebook and opened it. I saw many drawings of animals and birds.

'These creatures all live in the Amazon forest,' said the Professor.

I turned a page. I saw a picture of a strange landscape. There was a long line of dark red cliffs. The cliffs rose up from the ground and made a plateau at the top. The plateau was flat and very high off the ground. There were trees and green plants on top.

'What a strange place,' I said. 'Where is it?'

The Professor did not reply. I turned another page and cried out in surprise. 'Good God!' I said. 'What's this?'

It was a picture of a very strange and wonderful animal. It had the head of a snake and the body of a lizard. Its body and long tail had many sharp spikes.

'It's like a creature from a bad dream,' I said.

'No,' said the Professor. 'I think it's real. It's a picture of a living animal.'

I stared at the drawing. I did not understand. What did the Professor mean?

'Real?' I said. 'But how …?'

The Professor took a large book from his shelves. It was a book about dinosaurs – creatures from long ago. The book had many drawings of dinosaurs. The Professor pointed to one of them.

'Look at this drawing,' he said.

The drawing in the book looked like Maple White's drawing. I was sure it was the same creature. Beside the drawing in the book was written the name *stegosaurus*.

'It looks like the same animal!' I cried.

'Listen,' said the Professor. 'I spoke to the Indians. I asked them questions about Maple White. I asked them where he had been. They were very frightened, but they answered me.

'The next day, I went to find where Maple White had been. After many days, I came to the plateau in Maple White's drawing.'

'You found the same plateau!' I said.

'Yes,' said the Professor. 'I took a photograph. Here it is.'

He showed me a photograph. The photograph was not very good. But it showed the high line of cliffs. I was sure it was the same place.

I looked again at the photograph. Beside the cliffs there was a tall thin rock. This rock stood by itself. It was not joined to the cliffs. On top of the rock was a large tree. Something was sitting on the tree. It looked like a huge bird with a long beak.

'What's that bird?' I asked.

'It isn't a bird,' said the Professor. 'Look at this.'

He turned to another page in the dinosaur book. He showed me a picture of another creature. This creature looked like the one in the photograph. It looked like a bird. But it was not a bird. It had wings and a long, sharp beak with cruel teeth. Beside the drawing was written the name *pterodactyl*.

I was very excited. 'This is wonderful, Professor Challenger!' I said. 'You have found a place which no one knows about – a lost world. A world where creatures from the past still live.'

'But nobody in London believes my story,' said the Professor. His voice was angry and sad. 'Everyone says the drawing and the photograph are fakes – they aren't real.

'I want to return to the Lost World and climb up to the plateau. Maple White, the American, climbed up there. He drew the picture of the stegosaurus. So there must be a way up to the plateau.

'But other people must see the Lost World. Then everybody will know it is real.

'Mr Malone, tonight there is an important meeting at the Zoological Institute. I'm going to talk about the Lost World. Will you come to the meeting?'

'Of course, Professor,' I said. 'I'll be very happy to come.'

3
Our Journey Begins

The meeting at the Zoological Institute began at half past eight. The meeting hall was very crowded. Many famous professors and scientists were there. There were also many young students.

At the front of the hall there was a wide platform. The platform was higher than the people sitting in the audience. Some important scientists were sitting on the platform. I could see Professor Challenger.

A man called Mr Waldron was giving a talk. Mr Waldron was a famous scientist. His talk was called 'How Life on Earth Began'. It was very interesting. First he talked about how the earth was made. Then he talked about the first plants and animals. Then he talked about dinosaurs.

'All the dinosaurs are dead,' said Mr Waldron. 'All these creatures died millions of years ago.'

'Excuse me,' said a loud voice. 'That is not true.'

Mr Waldron was very surprised. He looked around.

'Who said that?' he asked.

'I did,' said Professor Challenger.

'What do you mean, Professor Challenger?' said Mr Waldron. He was very angry.

'The dinosaurs are not all dead,' said Professor Challenger. 'Some are still living.'

Some people began to laugh. But Mr Waldron did not laugh.

'And how do you know this, Professor?' he said coldly.

'I know this because I've seen them,' replied Professor Challenger. 'I've seen living dinosaurs.'

'Nonsense!' said Mr Waldron. 'The dinosaurs are all dead.

They died a long time ago. Please, Professor, let me finish my talk.'

But Professor Challenger wanted to talk to the people himself.

'I'm telling the truth,' he said. 'Two years ago I went to South America. I found a Lost World. Dinosaurs are living there. But nobody in London believes my story.

'So now I have an idea. Other people must go to South America to visit the Lost World. Then everybody will know my story is true. I ask you now. Who will go to South America to find the Lost World?'

The meeting hall was very quiet. Nobody spoke.

'I ask you again,' shouted Professor Challenger. 'Who will go and find the Lost World?'

A tall man wearing glasses stood up. His name was Professor Summerlee. He was a famous scientist.

'Professor Challenger, I don't believe your story,' said Professor Summerlee. 'But I'm a scientist too. It's my job to find out about things. So I'll go to South America. I'll find out if you are telling the truth.'

'Good,' said Professor Challenger. 'Who else will go?'

Then I made a decision. I decided to go to South America. I wanted to see the Lost World myself.

I stood up. At the same time, a tall thin man stood up too.

'I will go,' I said. 'My name is Edward Malone. I'm a reporter on the *Daily Gazette*.'

'And I will go,' said the tall thin man. 'My name is Lord John Roxton. I'm not a scientist. I'm a traveller. I'm an expert on South America. I've been there many times. I know the Amazon forest well.'

'Good,' said Professor Challenger. 'All these men will go to South America. They will find out the truth.'

'Good,' said Professor Challenger. 'All these men will go to South America. They will find out the truth.'

The audience shouted and cheered. The meeting was finished and soon I was outside in the street. A cold wind was blowing on my face.

What had I done? Had I made a terrible mistake? The journey to the Lost World would be very dangerous. I began to feel afraid.

Somebody touched my arm. It was the tall thin man from the meeting – Lord John Roxton.

'Come with me,' said Lord Roxton. 'I live near here. Come to my home and let's talk.'

Lord John Roxton's house was very interesting. He loved travelling. He had collected beautiful things from many countries. His house was full of carpets, pictures and furniture from all over the world.

Lord Roxton liked sport and he also enjoyed hunting. I saw the heads of many animals on the walls. Large and dangerous animals. Lord Roxton had hunted these animals and killed them.

I had heard many things about Lord Roxton. I knew he was a very brave man. Lord Roxton was not afraid of anything.

Lord Roxton was about thirty-eight years old. He had a strong body and cold blue eyes. He began to talk to me about South America. When he talked, I did not feel afraid any more. I felt strong and brave like him.

'I love South America,' said Lord Roxton. 'It's the most exciting country in the world.

'Perhaps the Professor's story is true. Perhaps there are dinosaurs in a Lost World.'

Later that evening I went to see Mr McArdle, my boss at the *Daily Gazette*. I told him everything that had happened.

'So you are going to look for Professor Challenger's Lost

World,' said Mr McArdle. 'Well, Malone, you are going to have an adventure. Good luck to you.'

'Thank you, Mr McArdle,' I said. 'I'll send reports about my journey to the *Daily Gazette*.'

Before we left England, Professor Challenger gave Professor Summerlee, Lord Roxton and me an envelope.

'There is a town by the River Amazon called Manaos,' he said. 'When you reach Manaos, open this envelope. You must open it on 15th July at twelve o'clock. I have written some instructions inside. The instructions will tell you how to find the Lost World.'

Ten days later, at the beginning of May, Professor Summerlee, Lord Roxton and I left for South America. We sailed on a ship called the *Francisca*.

And so we began our difficult and dangerous journey. But was there a Lost World? Would we find it? I did not know.

4

The River Amazon

After many weeks of travelling, we reached the town of Manaos on the River Amazon.

There were many Indians living near Manaos. These Indians knew Lord Roxton very well. When they saw him, they became very excited.

'Why are the Indians so pleased to see you?' I asked Lord Roxton.

'Five years ago,' he replied, 'a man called Pedro Lopez was living here. Lopez was of mixed race – his mother was an Indian and his father was a Mexican. Lopez was very rich.

He owned a lot of land. Many Indians worked for Lopez on his land. But he gave them very little money or food. Lopez was a terrible man. The work was very hard and many Indians died.

'I saw that Lopez was very cruel. I fought him and killed him. The Indians were very happy because I killed Lopez.'

We needed many things for our journey. We needed guns, tents, food and blankets. All these things were very heavy. We could not carry them ourselves. We needed some servants to help us.

We found some very good men. They were five Indians and two men of mixed race. One of the Indians was tall and strong. He was called Sancho. The two men of mixed race were called Gomez and Miguel. Gomez spoke very good English.

At twelve o'clock on 15th July, Professor Summerlee, Lord Roxton and I sat round a table. We were going to open Professor Challenger's envelope. Lord Roxton opened the envelope and a piece of paper fell out. I picked it up and turned it over. We looked at it in surprise. The paper was blank. There was nothing written on it at all.

Professor Summerlee was very angry. 'I knew it!' he said. 'Challenger is playing games with us. There is no Lost World. It's a trick. I'm going back to London.'

'May I come in?' said a loud voice.

A man came into the room – a short man with a long black beard and an enormous head.

'Professor Challenger!' we all cried.

'Yes,' said Professor Challenger. 'I'm sorry I tricked you but I wanted to surprise you. I'm coming with you to the Lost World.'

Lord Roxton and I were very pleased. Now we would find

the plateau easily. But Summerlee said nothing. He was not happy to see Professor Challenger. He did not like Challenger's trick. And he did not believe in the Lost World.

The next day, we left Manaos. We sailed up the Amazon in a boat called the *Esmerelda*. After four days, we left the Amazon and sailed up a smaller river. There was an Indian village beside this river. The Indians in this village had fine canoes. These canoes were long thin boats with paddles.

We bought two canoes from the Indians in the village. Then for two days we paddled up the river in our canoes.

On each side of the river there were thick forests with tall trees. The branches of the trees grew out over the river. The forest on both sides of the river was very dark. We could not see into the forest. We could not see any animals. But we heard birds and monkeys in the tree branches high above us.

Professor Challenger and Professor Summerlee were scientists. So they were very interested in the living things in the forest. They watched each plant and insect. They listened to the birds. But they could not agree with each other about anything. They argued all the time.

In the afternoon of the next day, Professor Challenger suddenly cried out, 'There it is! The way to the Lost World!'

I saw an opening on one side of the river. Some tall green plants grew across this opening. We pushed our canoes through the plants and came to a small stream.

This stream was a wonderful place. The water was bright and clear and we could see many beautiful fish. Near the stream there were brightly coloured animals and birds. They were not afraid of us at all.

'There it is!' the Professor cried out.
'The way to the Lost World!'

We paddled our canoes up the stream for three days. Then the stream became very narrow. We could not take our canoes any further. We left them under some trees beside the stream and started to walk.

We walked for nine days. We carried everything on our backs. Our journey was very difficult. Sometimes the ground was dry and rocky. Sometimes it was very soft and wet. Sometimes huge plants were in our way and we had to cut them down. We were walking up and up.

On the ninth day, we saw a line of high cliffs in front of us. The cliffs were dark red. They were flat at the top and made a plateau.

I knew the place at once. Professor Challenger had shown me Maple White's drawing in London. The plateau was in the drawing. Now we could all see the plateau. We had reached the plateau of the Lost World.

5

A Terrible Thing Happens

That night, we camped under the high red cliffs below the plateau. We put up our tents and made a fire to cook some food.

Near our camp was a tall thin rock. There was a tree growing on top of the rock. I remembered this rock. Professor Challenger had shown me a photograph in London. The cliffs, and the rock were in the photograph.

The rock was not joined to the cliffs. Between the rock and the cliffs was an abyss – a wide empty space.

The next morning after breakfast we had a meeting.

'How can we get up to the plateau?' I asked. 'The cliffs

are very high. We cannot climb them.'

'Perhaps there is no way up,' said Professor Summerlee.

'I'm sure there is,' said Professor Challenger. I think Maple White, the American, found a way up. He drew a picture of an animal he found there – a stegosaurus. I believe the stegosaurus was on top of the plateau. There must be a way up.'

'Let's walk round the plateau,' said Lord Roxton. 'The plateau is like a huge circle. We can walk all round the bottom of the cliffs. Then we'll find the way up.'

We started walking. The walk was very difficult. The ground was covered with broken rocks. After a time we stopped. We saw some things on the ground. There were some empty tins and bottles and an old newspaper too.

'Somebody has camped in this place,' said Lord Roxton.

'Yes,' said Professor Challenger. 'The newspaper is American. So this must be Maple White's camp.'

A tree was growing beside the camp. A small piece of wood was fixed on the tree. The wood was shaped like an arrow. It was pointing to the west.

'Look!' said Lord Roxton. 'Maple White made a sign. The sign shows us the way to go. Come on!'

We walked for a long time. Then we came to a narrow opening in the cliffs. We saw another arrow. It pointed towards the opening.

'This way!' said Lord Roxton.

Soon we were at the entrance to a cave. We climbed up to the cave. It led into a long dark tunnel. We started to walk along the tunnel. Lord Roxton was in front. Suddenly he stopped.

'The roof has fallen in,' he said. 'The tunnel is blocked by rocks. Maple White's way up to the plateau is closed.'

We did not know what to do. We were very tired. So we decided to go back to our camp. We did not speak much. But we were all thinking the same thing. Maple White's way was closed. So how could we get up to the plateau?

That night a very strange thing happened.

Lord Roxton had shot an animal – a small deer. We had made a fire and were cooking the deer for dinner. We were hungry and the meat smelt good.

Suddenly something came out of the dark night sky. I saw a terrible creature with huge wings. It had red eyes and a neck like a snake. It had a long beak with many sharp teeth.

The creature flew over our camp. The next minute it had gone. So had our dinner.

'It's taken our meat!' said Lord Roxton.

Professor Summerlee was staring at the dark sky. He turned to Professor Challenger. 'Challenger,' he said quietly. 'I'm very sorry. I didn't believe your stories about the Lost World. But now I believe you. That frightening creature was a pterodactyl.'

'Good, Summerlee,' said Professor Challenger.

The two Professors shook hands. For the first time, they were friends.

―――

The next morning, I was woken by Professor Challenger. He was shouting and waving his arms. He looked very happy.

'What is it?' I said.

'Get up, everybody!' he shouted. 'I've found the answer to our problem. I know how we can get onto the plateau.'

'How?' we all asked.

Professor Challenger pointed to the tall rock with the tree on top.

'We must climb to the top of that rock,' he said.

We looked at each other. We did not understand.

'But,' said Professor Summerlee, 'there is an abyss between the rock and the plateau. I don't understand …'

'Don't ask questions,' said Professor Challenger. 'Do as I say.'

We climbed up the rock. Gomez and Miguel came with us. They carried our guns. Sancho waited down on the ground below, with the other Indians.

At last, we stood beside the tree on top of the tall rock. Now we could see across to the plateau. A thick dark forest was growing there. But the abyss was between us and the plateau.

'Now – tell us, Challenger,' said Professor Summerlee. 'How can we cross the abyss?'

Professor Challenger smiled. He put his hand on the tree. 'This tree will help us,' he said.

'Of course!' said Lord Roxton. 'A bridge!'

'Yes,' said Professor Challenger. 'Malone is the youngest and strongest. He can cut down the tree. The tree will fall across the abyss like a bridge. Then we can cross to the plateau.'

'That's a wonderful idea,' Summerlee said.

Professor Challenger had brought an axe. He gave it to me. I began to cut down the tree. At last it fell. It fell across the abyss with a loud crash.

Now we had a bridge to the Lost World.

'Let me go across first,' said Professor Challenger.

He sat down on the tree and slowly moved across. Soon he was standing on the plateau.

'At last! At last!' he cried.

Professor Summerlee went next. Then it was my turn. I did not want to look down at the ground far below. Lord Roxton was the last one to cross the bridge. Soon we all stood on the plateau. All around were small trees and thick bushes. Each man carried his gun on his back.

Gomez and Miguel did not come with us. They stayed behind on the rock.

Professor Challenger pointed straight ahead. 'Let's go that way,' he said.

We began to walk into the bushes. Then a terrible thing happened. We heard a loud crash. We turned and ran back to the edge of the plateau. We could not believe what we saw. The tree had gone! It had fallen into the abyss. It lay on the ground far below. Our bridge had gone. We could not leave the Lost World!

6

Creatures From the Past

What were we going to do? Summerlee, Challenger, Lord Roxton and I stood at the edge of the plateau. Now we could not escape from the Lost World.

Suddenly, we heard a shout. It came from across the abyss. Gomez was standing on top of the tall rock. He was shouting and waving his arms.

'Lord Roxton!' he shouted. 'Lord John Roxton!'

'Here I am,' said Lord Roxton.

'Yes, there you are,' shouted Gomez. 'And there you will stay. I've waited a long time for this moment.'

'What do you mean?' said Lord Roxton.

'Do you remember Pedro Lopez?' shouted Gomez. 'The man you killed five years ago? Well, Pedro Lopez was my brother. Now you are going to die. You and your friends will die in the Lost World. Goodbye, Lord Roxton!'

Then we understood. The tree had not fallen. Gomez had wanted to destroy our bridge. So he and Miguel had pushed the tree into the abyss.

Gomez started to climb down the rock to the ground. But he climbed slowly. Lord Roxton pointed his gun and fired. We heard a terrible scream. Then we saw Gomez's body falling to the ground below.

'Gomez is dead,' I said. 'But what about Miguel?'

'Look!' said Lord Roxton.

Miguel had reached the ground far below. He was running – running for his life. Behind him was Sancho, the tall Indian. We saw Sancho jump on Miguel. The two men fell to the ground. They fought. Then Sancho stood up. The other man did not move.

'Sancho has killed him,' said Lord Roxton. 'Now we must wait for Sancho to climb the rock.'

At last Sancho appeared on the top of the rock opposite the plateau.

'Some of the other Indians want to leave,' he said. 'They are afraid to stay in this terrible place. But I won't leave. I'll stay here and help you.'

Sancho brought many things from our camp to the top of the rock. Then he threw them across to the plateau. There were tins of food, bullets for our guns and many other things. Now we could camp for many days.

'Sancho,' said Lord Roxton. 'We want you to stay in the camp at the bottom of the rock. Tell one of the Indians to go back to the Indian village. Tell him to bring us long ropes so we can get down.'

Then I wrote a report for Mr McArdle. I threw it across to Sancho. 'Tell the Indian to take this with him. Tell him to send it to London,' I said.

We found a clearing – a space among the bushes and small trees. Then we made a camp. We put all our things together in the clearing. Then we cut many branches from the trees and bushes. We put the branches round our camp to make a wall. We began to feel safe.

'Let's go and explore the plateau,' said Lord Roxton. 'Let's find out what creatures live here.'

A small stream ran through the clearing. We began to walk beside the stream. It went into a forest. As we walked, we saw many beautiful birds and insects. There were also many strange trees and plants.

Lord Roxton was walking in front. Suddenly he stopped.

'Look at this!' he said.

The ground beside the stream was wet and muddy. I saw some enormous footprints in the mud. A huge animal had made these footprints. Some footprints showed three toes and some showed five toes.

'What creature has made these footprints?' asked Lord Roxton.

'The creature which made these footprints is very big,' said Professor Challenger. 'It is walking on two long legs with three big toes and two small front legs with five toes. I think these are the footprints of a dinosaur.'

We saw more and more footprints in the mud. We followed the footprints. At last we came to an open space in the trees. And there we saw a very strange sight.

In the clearing were three creatures. There were two adults and a baby. The baby was as big as an elephant. The adults were enormous. The creatures had long thick tails and feet with three big toes. They had very small arms with five fingers on the hands. Their skin was shiny and grey.

The creatures were pulling down branches from the trees with their hands and eating the leaves. We watched them for a long time. We could not believe what we were seeing. At last the creatures moved away.

'What are they?' said Lord Roxton.

'They are *iguanodons*,' said Professor Challenger. 'Long ago many iguanodons lived in England. They ate trees and plants. But the trees and plants they needed disappeared. So there was no more food and they died. Here they can find their food. So the iguanodons are alive.'

We walked on through the forest. At last we came to a line of tall rocks. From behind the rocks came a very strange noise. It was like the hissing of many snakes. Then I noticed something else. There was a horrible smell.

We walked forward very slowly and quietly. Then we looked over the top of the rocks.

We were looking down into a huge pit. The pit was

The creatures were pulling down branches from the trees with their hands and eating the leaves.

shaped like a bowl. The sides of the pit were covered with mud. At the bottom were pools of dirty green water.

In the pit were hundreds of pterodactyls. The females were sitting on huge yellow eggs. There were babies beside the pools of green water. They were flapping their wings and hissing. Each male pterodactyl sat on a stone. Their long grey wings were folded and they did not move at all. They waited and watched with their red eyes.

It was a horrible sight. I felt sick because of the smell. But Professor Challenger was very interested in the pterodactyls. He tried to move closer.

At once a pterodactyl saw him. It flapped its wings and flew into the air with a loud cry. Other pterodactyls followed. They flew in a circle high in the sky. Then they flew down towards us. They were going to attack.

'Run!' shouted Lord Roxton. 'Run to the trees!'

We ran as fast as we could. But we were too late. The pterodactyls began to attack us with their beaks. Professor Summerlee cried out. I saw blood running down his face. I felt a sharp pain in the back of my neck.

Professor Challenger fell. At once, the pterodactyls were on him. Then I heard the loud crash of a gun.

Lord Roxton had shot a pterodactyl. The others flew away. We picked up Professor Challenger and ran back into the forest. We were safe there. The pterodactyls' wings were huge. They could not fly between the trees.

We went slowly back to our camp. We needed to rest. My neck was very painful.

Someone or something had been in our camp. The wall of branches around our camp was not broken. But inside the wall many things were broken. Tins were smashed open. The food inside was gone. Who or what had done this?

We looked around. Everything was very quiet. The forest

was dark. We could see nothing but I felt frightened. I knew someone or something was watching us.

7
Death in the Night

The next day, we stayed in our camp all day. We cut down more branches from the trees and used them to make a stronger wall around the camp. All day, I thought that someone was watching us. But I saw nothing.

That night – our second night in the Lost World – we heard a dreadful noise. We were sleeping by our fire. Suddenly we were woken by a loud cry. It came from very near our camp.

More cries and screams followed. They were terrible to hear. They were the screams of an animal. An animal in great pain.

I put my hands over my ears. But I could still hear the terrible screams. The screams went on for a few minutes. Then they stopped. There was silence in the forest.

'What was it?' I whispered.

'We'll find out in the morning,' said Lord Roxton. 'The sounds were very close to us.'

'Listen!' said Professor Summerlee. 'Something is coming towards our camp.'

We listened. We heard the heavy footsteps of a large animal. Something was walking round the camp. Then it stopped. We picked up our guns.

Lord Roxton looked out through the wall of branches.

'I can see it!' he said.

I went and stood next to him. I saw a large black shape in

the shadow of the trees. I heard a loud hiss. Then I saw two terrible green eyes. The creature was moving forward.

'It's going to attack us!' I said.

Then Lord Roxton did a very brave thing. He picked up a burning branch from the fire. He ran out of the camp towards the creature. The light of the burning branch was bright. I saw a horrible face. The creature had the head of a very large lizard. There was blood on its mouth and on its sharp teeth.

Lord Roxton pushed the burning branch into the huge creature's face. The creature turned away in fear. The next moment it had gone.

The next morning, we found a dead iguanodon near our camp. Its body was torn into many pieces. There was blood everywhere.

'This iguanodon was killed by the terrible creature we saw last night,' said Professor Challenger. 'The creature was a very large meat-eating dinosaur – an *allosaurus*, or perhaps a *megalosaurus*.'

Lord Roxton was looking carefully at the leg of the dead iguanodon.

'What's this mark on the skin?' he asked. 'It's very strange.'

There was a large black circle on the shiny skin of the iguanodon.

'It looks like tar. And its sticky,' said Professor Summerlee. 'So there must be tar on the plateau. But how did it get onto the iguanodon's skin?'

All day we walked in the forest. We found lovely flowers and plants. There were also trees with delicious fruit.

We saw some more iguanodons. They also had tar circles on their skin. What did these marks mean?

In the camp that evening, Lord Roxton said, 'What shall we do tomorrow?'

'We have seen enough of the Lost World,' replied Professor Summerlee. 'Now we must think how to leave it.'

'What, Summerlee!' shouted Professor Challenger. 'We are scientists. We must find out more things about this wonderful place.'

'No,' said Professor Summerlee. 'The Lost World is very interesting. But it's also very dangerous. We must leave now. The dinosaurs will kill us. Then nobody in London will ever hear the whole story.'

Professor Challenger thought for a long time.

'You're right, Summerlee,' he said at last. 'We must return to London. But I want a map of the Lost World. I want to show it to people at home.'

Then I had a wonderful idea. A huge tree was growing near our camp. When I was a boy, I was very good at climbing trees.

'Let me climb that tree,' I said. 'I'll be able to see the whole plateau from the top. Then I can draw a map.'

My friends were very pleased with my idea. So I began to climb the tree. The climb was not difficult. But the branches and leaves were very thick. I could not see the sky above my head.

Suddenly I had a terrible shock. A face was staring at me! It was an ugly face – like a human and like an ape. Its eyes were cruel and its mouth had long sharp teeth.

For a few seconds, the Ape-Man and I stared at each other. Then the face was gone. A red hairy body moved away through the leaves.

At last I reached the top of the tree. From there I saw a wonderful sight. It was late and the sun was setting. In the golden light, I could see the whole plateau far below. There

*Suddenly I had a terrible shock. A face
was staring at me!*

was a large lake in the centre of the plateau. It was green and beautiful in the evening light. On the far side of the lake was a line of red cliffs. In the cliffs there were some dark holes. They looked like caves.

It was beginning to get dark. I took a notebook out of my pocket and drew a map of the plateau. Then I climbed down the tree again.

My friends were very pleased to see me. I showed them my map. Then I told them about the Ape-Man.

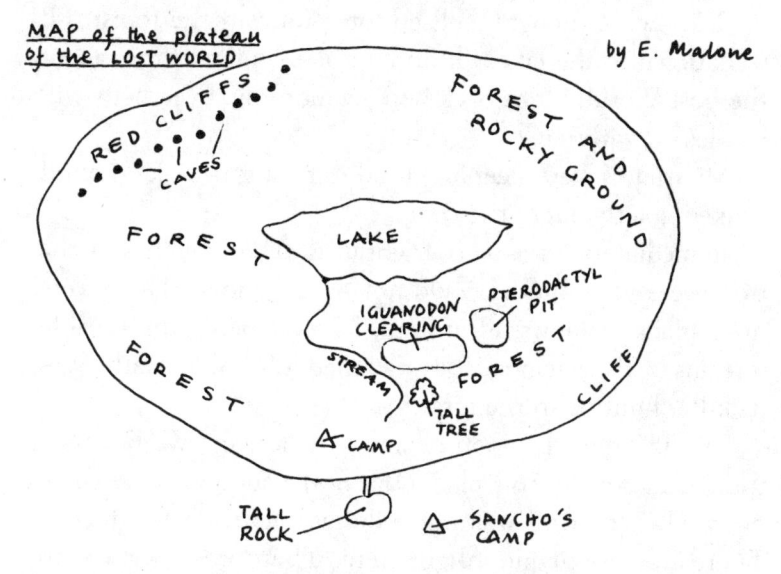

MAP of the plateau of the LOST WORLD — by E. Malone

RED CLIFFS • CAVES
FOREST AND ROCKY GROUND
FOREST
LAKE
IGUANODON CLEARING
PTERODACTYL PIT
STREAM
FOREST
TALL TREE
CLIFF
CAMP
TALL ROCK
SANCHO'S CAMP

'He has been watching us from that tree,' I said. 'When we were away, he came to our camp. I am sure he broke our things.'

'Now do you understand, Challenger?' said Professor Summerlee. 'We are not safe here. There are dangers all around. We must make plans to leave.'

'Yes,' said Professor Challenger. 'Malone, you have done well. Now we have a good map of the Lost World. Tomorrow, I promise I will think of a way to get down.'

8
A Dreadful Walk

That night, I could not sleep. I had helped my friends. Now they had a map of the Lost World. They were very pleased with me. I was very pleased with myself.

It was a beautiful night. There were hundreds of stars and a bright moon in the sky. The air was clear and cold.

'I know!' I thought. 'I'll go for a walk in the forest. I'll walk down to the lake. I'll find out many more things about the Lost World. I'll be back here by morning. Everybody will be pleased with me.'

My friends were sleeping. I did not want to wake them. I walked quietly out of the camp.

Immediately I was very frightened. The branches of the trees were very thick. I could not see the moon. There were huge black shadows all around. I remembered the terrible screams of the iguanodon. It had died a horrible death. Was its killer hunting in the forest now?

I walked quickly. Soon I came to a clearing. We had seen the iguanodons in this place. But no iguanodons were there now. The clearing was more dangerous than the forest. There was bright moonlight here. There was nowhere to hide. I ran quickly across the clearing and came to the stream on the other side. I knew the stream went down to the lake. So I followed it.

I passed the place of the pterodactyls. Suddenly a large pterodactyl flew into the air. It flew in front of the moon. It was a dark and horrible shape in the sky. At last it came down to the ground again. It had not seen me.

I will never forget that dreadful walk. Many times I heard the sounds of animals in the forest. My mouth was dry and my heart was beating fast in fear.

At last I reached the lake. I looked at my watch. It was one o'clock in the morning. I was very thirsty. I drank some cold fresh water from the lake. Then I lay down on top of a rock and looked around.

From this rock, I could see in every direction. Then I had a great surprise.

When I had climbed the tree in the afternoon, I had seen a line of cliffs. The cliffs had dark holes in them. The holes looked like caves. Now I could see the same cliffs again. They were on the other side of the lake. There were small circles of red light in the cliffs. The circles of red light were fires. But animals did not light fires. Only humans could make fire. There must be humans on the plateau! They were living in the caves. I stared in surprise.

The lake shone like glass in the moonlight. It was very beautiful. Sometimes I saw the head of a strange animal in the water. Everything was very quiet. I looked at the lake for a long time.

At half past two, I decided to return to the camp. I started to walk back through the forest. Then suddenly I heard a noise behind me. It was the noise of a large animal.

I ran across a moonlit clearing. Then I heard the sound again. This time it was louder and nearer. My skin was cold and my heart was beating fast. Was something following me?

I turned and looked behind me. Then suddenly I saw it. A huge black creature was coming out of the dark trees. It moved forward into the moonlight.

Was it an iguanodon? No. It had the head of a huge lizard and an enormous body. It had small arms and many long, sharp teeth. It was the most terrible meat-eating dinosaur of all. It was a *tyrannosaurus rex*. And it was hunting me.

I started to run. I ran and ran. At last I could run no

further. My legs were hurting and I was very tired.

I stopped. Everything was quiet. Suddenly there was a crashing sound in the trees. The creature had found me. I had not escaped!

The bright moonlight shone on the animal's huge eyes and its terrible sharp teeth. I screamed in terror and ran away. The dinosaur was close behind me. There was no escape.

Then suddenly there was a crash. I was falling, falling, and everything was darkness.

A few minutes later, I opened my eyes. Where was I? I smelt a horrible smell. I put out my hand. I felt the body of an animal.

Above me was a circle of sky. The moon was shining brightly. I could not see the tyrannosaurus. Moonlight was shining down on me and I looked around. I had fallen into a deep pit. There were the bodies of animals on the floor of the pit. In the middle of the pit was a tall wooden post. This stake had a sharp point on the top.

Now I understood. I had fallen into a trap. A trap for dinosaurs. Men had made this trap. They had covered the trap with branches. When the dinosaurs fell in, they died on the sharp stake.

There was no sound from above. I climbed out of the pit and looked around. I was still frightened. But the terrible dinosaur had gone.

The sky was getting lighter. It was almost dawn. My friends would be worried about me. I started walking towards the camp. At last I reached the stream. Suddenly I heard the sound of a gun. It came from the camp. I began to run.

At last I was at the camp. I shouted for my friends but there was no reply. I ran inside the wall of branches. In the morning sunshine I saw a terrible sight.

All our things lay broken on the ground. My friends had gone. The food had gone too but the guns were there. There was blood on the ground in the middle of the camp.

I ran outside the camp and called for my friends. But there was no answer. I did not know what to do. I did not know what to think. What had happened? Were my friends dead? Was I now alone in the Lost World? I felt sick with fear.

Suddenly I heard a shout. It was our servant, Sancho. He was calling me from the top of the rock. I ran to the edge of the plateau and looked across. I was very happy to see Sancho. Now I was not alone.

I told Sancho what had happened. He looked very worried.

'You must leave that terrible place at once,' he said.

'But how, Sancho?' I said. 'How can I get down?'

'The Indian we sent to the Indian village has not returned,' said Sancho. 'I'll send another man to the village to get ropes. I'll throw them across to make a bridge. Then you can get down.'

9

Prisoners of the Ape-People

My friends did not return that day. When night came, I was very tired. I lit a fire in the camp and went to sleep.

In the early morning I awoke. I felt a hand on my arm. Immediately I reached for my gun. Then I cried out in surprise. Lord Roxton was standing beside me.

Lord Roxton's face was white and his eyes were staring. His clothes were dirty and torn.

'Quick, Malone!' he said. 'Get all the guns and follow me. We must hurry. Come on!'

Soon I was running after Lord Roxton through the forest. I carried a gun in each hand. At last, we came to some very thick bushes. Lord Roxton rushed into the bushes and pulled me down beside him.

'We'll be safe here,' he said. 'They'll look for me in the camp first.'

I did not understand.

'Who are "they"?' I said. 'Who are we hiding from? And

where are the professors?'

'The Ape-People have got them,' replied Lord Roxton. 'My God, what terrible creatures! But where did you go, Malone?'

I told Lord Roxton about my walk to the lake. I told him about the fires I had seen in the cliffs. Then I told him about the terrible dinosaur and the pit with the sharp stake.

'There must be humans on the plateau,' I said. 'Only humans could make fire and the dinosaur pit.'

'I know,' said Lord Roxton. 'I've seen them.'

'You've seen the humans!' I said. 'Where?'

'Listen,' said Lord Roxton. 'Let me tell you the whole story. The Ape-People attacked our camp early yesterday morning. They came down out of the trees. I shot one of them in the stomach. But the Ape-People were very strong. We could not fight them all.

'They tied our hands behind our backs and sat in a circle around us. They are strange creatures. Their arms are long but their legs are short. They have grey eyes and thick red hair.

'We didn't know what the Ape-People were going to do. At last, Challenger stood up and shouted at them. Then we saw a very strange thing. One of the Ape-People came and stood beside Challenger. This Ape-Man was their king.

'We couldn't believe what we saw. The Ape-King and Challenger looked like brothers! They both had short bodies, strong arms and large heads. But the colour of their hair was different. Challenger's hair was black and the Ape-King's hair was red.

'The Ape-People stared too. Then they began to laugh. They thought it was very funny. At last, they took us through the forest. The Ape-People pulled Summerlee and me through the bushes. But they carried Challenger high on their shoulders like a king.

'They took us to their town. They live in houses near the edge of the plateau. Summerlee and I were prisoners. Our hands and feet were tied together. But Challenger was taken up into a tree. He ate fruit with the Ape-King.

'Then more Ape-People arrived. They had brought some new prisoners – humans. The prisoners were small Indian men.'

'So those Indians must live in the caves by the lake,' I said.

'Yes,' said Lord Roxton. 'All the Ape-People were looking at the new prisoners. I knew this was my chance to escape. At last I was able to untie my hands and feet. I ran through the forest to our camp.'

'But what about the professors?' I cried.

'We must go back and help them,' said Lord Roxton. 'But we need guns to fight the Ape-People. That's why I came back to the camp – to get the guns.'

Suddenly Lord Roxton stopped talking. 'Listen!' he said.

I heard a strange clicking noise. I saw dark shapes moving through the forest.

'The Ape-People!' whispered Lord Roxton. 'That's how they talk to each other. They're looking for us.'

We waited. When all the Ape-People had passed us we walked slowly out of the bushes.

'The forest is very dangerous,' said Lord Roxton. 'The Ape-People move through the branches of the trees. They can watch us but we can't see them. We can run faster on the ground than the Ape-People. Let's stay out of the forest. We will be safer in the clearings.'

At last we were near the Ape-Town. We crept forwards through long grass and watched.

A wide open space was in front of us. There were small

houses in the open space. They were built of branches and leaves. A huge crowd of Ape-People stood in front of the houses. They were all watching something at the cliff at the edge of the plateau. Watching and waiting.

There was a group of five Indians by the cliff. A tall man stood beside them. It was Professor Summerlee.

Then I saw Professor Challenger. He was standing beside the Ape-King. Lord Roxton was right. Challenger and the Ape-King looked like brothers.

The Ape-King moved his hand. Two Ape-Men ran forward and took hold of one of the Indians. They pulled him to the cliff and threw him over the edge. The crowd of Ape-People ran forward. They shouted and cheered.

At last they were quiet. The Ape-King moved his hand again. This time the Ape-People took hold of Professor Summerlee.

I saw Challenger point at Summerlee and speak to the Ape-King. But the king shook his head. The Ape-People began to pull Summerlee towards the cliff.

Then I heard the crash of a gun. The Ape-King fell dead. Lord Roxton had shot him.

'Malone – shoot, shoot!' Lord Roxton cried.

I shot at the crowd of Ape-People. They could not understand what was happening. I killed some of them and the others ran to the trees. Challenger, Summerlee and the four Indians were left by the cliff.

Challenger took hold of Summerlee's arm and the two men ran towards us. We ran through the forest to our camp. The Ape-People did not follow us. They were afraid of our guns. We ran into our camp and we pulled the wall of branches together behind us. Then we heard cries. The four Indian prisoners stood outside our wall. They had followed us through the forest.

The Ape-People began to pull Summerlee towards the cliff.

'We must help these poor men,' said Professor Challenger. 'But where do they live?'

'I know,' I said. 'They live in the caves on the other side of the lake.'

'Let's go there tomorrow,' said Lord Roxton.

10

The Battle

That night we all slept well. We were safe in our camp. Next morning, we started our journey to the Indian caves. We decided to go across the plateau and round the lake.

We walked through the forest. The four Indians went in front, then the two Professors. Lord Roxton and I were at the back, carrying guns. But we did not see any Ape-People.

The Indians were small and strong with kind, friendly faces. I liked them very much. They talked to each other but we could not understand their language. One of the Indians was a young man. He walked in front of the others and he told them what to do. Perhaps he was a prince or young king.

'How did the Indians get onto the plateau?' asked Lord Roxton.

'I think the dinosaurs and the Ape-People were living on the plateau first,' replied Professor Challenger. The Indians came later. They came up to the plateau from below – perhaps they came the same way as Maple White. Perhaps they were looking for food.

'They decided to live in the caves. They are safe from dinosaurs there. The dinosaurs are too large to enter the caves. So the Ape-People are the Indians' worst enemies.'

Professor Summerlee shook his head. 'No, Challenger,' he said. 'I don't agree with you. I think …'

But I was not listening to Professor Summerlee. I saw something move in the trees above me. I jumped back quickly but I was too late.

Two long red arms had come down from the trees. Two huge hairy hands closed round my neck and face. Strong hands lifted me from the ground.

I could not cry out. A horrible face was looking down at me. A face with cruel grey eyes and big teeth. I could not move. I could not breathe. From far away I heard the sound of a gun. Then I was dropped on the ground and everything went dark.

I was woken by Lord Roxton. He was washing my face with cold water. The two professors stood nearby.

'Thank God you are all right, Malone!' said Lord Roxton. 'We thought you were dead. An Ape-Man had caught you. He dropped you when I shot at him.'

Now we knew that the Ape-People were watching us. We hurried on through the forest. In the late afternoon we reached the lake. The Indians gave a cry of joy and pointed to the water.

We saw a wonderful sight. Many canoes were coming towards us across the lake. In the canoes there were Indians. They were carrying spears and bows and arrows.

The canoes reached the edge of the lake and the Indians got out. They ran towards us. One of them was an old man. He wore clothes made of animal skins and a necklace of large beads. He put his arms round the young Indian.

'So the young man is the son of the chief,' said Lord Roxton.

The Indian chief asked his son many questions. They talked for a long time. Then he came and put his arms round each of us. He was very happy because his son was alive.

But the young prince became angry. Many times he pointed to the trees around us. He began to talk to his people. We could not understand his words. But we could understand what he wanted to do.

'My friends,' he was saying, 'we cannot return home. I am alive but others are dead. We will never be safe from our enemies, the Ape-People. So we must kill them now.'

He pointed to us. 'These strange men are our friends. They will help us. They hate the Ape-People too. Let us fight together against our enemies. Let us kill them or die.'

He finished speaking. The Indians shouted and cheered. They waved their spears in the air. They were ready to fight.

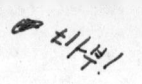

'They are very brave,' said Lord Roxton. 'I'm going to help them. I'm going to fight the Ape-People. Are you coming, Malone?'

'Of course,' I said.

'And I am too,' said Professor Challenger.

'What about you, Summerlee?' said Lord Roxton.

'I'm a scientist,' said Professor Summerlee. 'I'm not a fighter. But, yes, I'll come with you.'

'Good,' said Lord Roxton.

That evening we camped by the lake. The Indians lit fires. Then some of them went into the forest. When they came back, they had a young iguanodon with them.

The iguanodon had a tar circle on its skin. In a few minutes the iguanodon was killed. They cut up the meat and cooked it.

Now we understood. The Indians kept the iguanodons for meat. Each Indian owned some iguanodons. Each owner marked their iguanodons with special tar marks.

The two professors were very interested in the beautiful lake. They watched the water for many hours. Far out in the lake we saw many more strange creatures.

The next day, there was a terrible battle between the Ape-People and the Indians. In the open spaces the Indians were better fighters than the Ape-People. They could run faster than their enemies. They killed many Ape-People with their spears and bows and arrows.

But in the forest the Ape-People were better fighters than the Indians. They hid in the trees and attacked the Indians.

Again and again we fired our guns. We shot many Ape-People. At last the battle was finished and all the Ape-People were dead.

We went back to our first camp at the edge of the plateau. We called down to Sancho. He climbed up the tall rock. He had heard the noise of the battle.

'Come away from that terrible place,' he cried.

'Sancho is right,' said Professor Summerlee. 'Now, Challenger, remember your promise. Find a way for us to leave the Lost World. We have had enough adventures.'

11

Escape from the Lost World

The Ape-People were all dead and now we were safe. We started to make plans to escape form the Lost World.

We made a new camp below the Indian caves. The openings of these caves were very high up in the cliffs. There were narrow steps going up to them. No large animals could climb these steps. So the Indians were safe from dinosaurs. But on the ground the Indians were not safe.

One evening, we saw some Indians running away from two huge tyrannosaurs. The dinosaurs killed six Indians. But the dinosaurs could not get up to the caves. The Indians in the caves shot them with poisoned arrows.

We spent many interesting and wonderful days on the plateau. The tyrannosaurus rex usually hunted at night. So in the day we were safe. There was only one problem. We could not find a way to get down from the plateau. The Indians were helpful and friendly to us. But they would not help us to leave the Lost World.

'Perhaps the Indians don't want us to leave,' said Lord Roxton. 'We helped them fight the Ape-People. We brought them good luck. So they want us to stay here.'

One Indian understood why we were unhappy. We had saved him from the Ape-People. The young son of the chief wanted to help us.

One day, I went over to the other side of the plateau to see Sancho. None of the Indians had returned from the village with ropes.

'Don't worry,' said Sancho. 'I'm sure one of them will come back soon. Then you will be able to get down.'

On the way back to our camp near the caves, I passed near the pterodactyl pit. Suddenly I saw something very strange coming towards me. It looked like a cage with a man's legs. The cage was made of sticks. Inside the cage was a man. It was Lord Roxton. When he saw me, he laughed.

'What are you doing?' I asked him.

'I'm visiting the pterodactyls,' said Lord Roxton. 'I made this cage so that I will be safe.'

'Yes, but why do you want to go there?' I asked.

'I can't tell you now,' said Lord Roxton. 'Professor Challenger has asked me to do something, but it's a secret.'

'All right,' I said. 'But can't I help you?'

'No,' said Lord Roxton. 'I'm safe in this cage and you are not. I'll see you at the camp this evening.'

A few more days passed and we began to get very worried. We had not found a way to escape from the Lost World. Then one evening, we had a visitor to our camp. It was the chief's son. He gave me a small piece of the bark of a tree. The bark was like a piece of paper. On the bark there were some marks.

The young man pointed to the caves above our heads. Then he went quietly back to his people.

We looked at the marks on the piece of bark. They

Suddenly I saw something very strange coming towards me.
It looked like a cage with a man's legs.

looked like this:

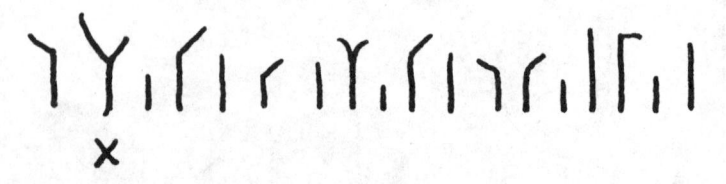

⁊Ẏıſ|ɾıẎ.ſ|⁊ɾı|ſı|
×

'I'm sure this is important,' I said. 'But what does it mean?'

'It looks like a map,' said Professor Summerlee.

'Look!' said Lord Roxton. 'There are eighteen marks on the bark. And how many caves are there? Eighteen. The young man has drawn us a map of the caves.'

'Yes,' I said. 'And there's a cross by one of the caves. Perhaps there is a way through that cave. Perhaps he is showing us the way out of the Lost World!'

We were all very excited. We picked up pieces of wood and climbed up to the cave. When we were inside the cave, we lit the pieces of wood. Now we had torches of fire. Now we could see in the darkness. We were in a long tunnel.

We walked along the tunnel for a long time. Then suddenly we saw a light in front of us. It was like silver fire. But no heat or sound came from the light.

'It's the moon!' shouted Lord Roxton. 'We have reached the other side of the cliff!'

Lord Roxton was right. There was a small opening in front of us and moonlight was shining through it. We pushed our heads out of the opening and felt the cool night air. The opening was like a tiny window. But a man could push his body through it. The ground was not far below the opening.

We went back to our camp and got ready to leave. We did not tell the Indians about our plans.

The next evening, we left the Lost World. As we climbed up to the cave, we saw the Indian fires below us. We heard the Indians talking and laughing. Then we heard the cry of a dinosaur in the forest. It was the last sound we heard as we left.

We carried all our things with us. One package was very heavy and difficult to carry. It belonged to Professor Challenger. Something very special was in this package.

At last we reached the bottom of the cliff. Soon we found Sancho's camp. The Indian servants had returned with twenty others. They had brought food and strong ropes. We did not need the ropes now but we were very happy to see them. The Indians would help us get back to the River Amazon.

12

We Return to London

We were very pleased to be back in our own world. But we were also sad. The Lost World was a very special place. Each of us had learned many things. We would never forget that strange and wonderful place.

We had an easy journey back to London. I had sent more reports about the Lost World to Mr McArdle, my boss at the *Daily Gazette*. People read my reports in the newspaper.

Two days after we got back to England there was a meeting at the Zoological Institute. This was the place where my adventures had began. This was where I first saw Professor Summerlee and Lord Roxton. So many things had happened since that time.

Now the meeting hall was crowded with hundreds of people. There were famous professors, scientists and many ordinary people too. Everyone had come to hear our story.

Professor Summerlee, Professor Challenger, Lord Roxton and I sat on a platform at the front of the hall. Professor Summerlee stood up to speak.

'Last year in this hall,' he said, 'Professor Challenger spoke about the Lost World. I did not believe his story. But now I have seen the Lost World myself. Everything he said is true.'

Professor Summerlee spoke for a long time. He told the people about our difficult journey to the plateau. He described the wonderful animals and plants. He spoke about the dinosaurs. He described the Ape-People and Indians.

At last he sat down. The meeting hall was quiet. Nobody knew what to think. Then a man stood up. He was a scientist called Dr Illingworth.

'A year ago,' said Dr Illingworth, 'one man – Professor Challenger – told us many things about a lost world. Now four men are telling us these same things.

'But perhaps these men want to be famous. Perhaps they are not telling the truth. Perhaps they are telling lies about the Lost World. How do we know there is a Lost World?

'Professor Challenger, you must show us some evidence from the Lost World. You must show us something which we can see ourselves. Then we will believe you.'

'Yes, yes. Dr Illingworth is right!' shouted the people in the audience. 'Show us something from the Lost World!'

Professor Challenger stood up. 'We have some very good photographs,' he said. 'We have a wonderful photograph of a pterodactyl.'

'No, no,' said Dr Illingworth. 'We don't want photographs. Maybe the photographs are fakes – maybe they aren't real.'

'So,' said Professor Challenger. 'You want to see something real. All right, then. What about a real pterodactyl? Will you believe us then?'

'Of course,' said Dr Illingworth. He laughed. 'Show us a live pterodactyl.'

The people in the audience laughed too. They were enjoying themselves.

But Professor Challenger did not laugh. 'All right,' he said. 'Bring me that box, Malone.' He pointed to the back of the platform.

I stood up and went to the back of the platform. I found a large box there and brought it to the professor. It was the heavy package that we had carried back from the Lost World.

Professor Challenger opened the box. There was a loud hissing sound from inside. A few seconds later, a creature stood on the edge of the box. It was a horrible creature with long wings, bright red eyes and a beak full of sharp teeth. It was a baby pterodactyl!

The people were shocked. For a moment there was silence. They looked at the horrible creature. Then somebody screamed. People tried to get out of their chairs and run away.

The noise frightened the pterodactyl. It flapped its wings and flew into the air. It began to fly around inside the hall. Now everybody was shouting and screaming. The baby pterodactyl became more and more afraid. It flew faster and faster. It was looking for a way to escape.

'Shut the windows!' shouted Professor Challenger.

But it was too late. The pterodactyl had found an open window and flew out.

At first nobody spoke. Then everybody began to shout and cheer. Now they knew our story was true. We were carried outside. Thousands more people were waiting in the streets. We were carried through London like heroes – men who had done great and good things.

But what happened to the pterodactyl? We do not know for sure. But next day, far out in the middle of the Atlantic Ocean, the captain of a ship saw a strange creature. It was a creature which looked like a huge flying lizard. It passed his ship and flew south-west across the Atlantic.

Was it the pterodactyl flying back to the Lost World? Did it reach its home? Or did it die in the Atlantic Ocean? We will never know the answer.

Points for Understanding

1

1 What was Edward Malone's job?
2 Why did Malone go to see Professor Challenger?
3 Describe Professor Challenger.
4 What happened when Malone met Professor Challenger?

2

1 Professor Challenger had been on a journey. Where did he go? Who did he meet?
2 Who was Maple White? What had he found?
3 What did Professor Challenger do after he had seen Maple White's drawings?
4 What was in the photograph Challenger took?
5 What did Challenger want to do next?

3

1 Why did the audience at the Zoological Institute begin to laugh at Professor Challenger?
2 Who said they would go to the Lost World?
3 What does Malone tell us about Lord Roxton?
4 Professor Challenger gave the explorers an envelope. What were his instructions?

4

1 Why were the Indians in Manaos pleased to see Lord Roxton?
2 Who went with the explorers to help them?
3 Why was Professor Summerlee very angry?
4 How many days did it take the explorers to get to the Lost World?
5 How did they get there?

5

1. Where did the explorers make their camp?
2. How did they find Maple White's way up to the plateau? What problem did they find?
3. What happened while the explorers were cooking their dinner?
4. The next morning Challenger had an idea. What was it?
5. Who went into the Lost World? Who stayed behind?
6. 'We began to walk into the bushes. Then a terrible thing happened.' What happened?

6

1. What had Gomez done? Why had he done it?
2. What did the explorers ask Sancho to do?
3. The explorers saw some footprints. What had made these footprints?
4. 'It was a horrible sight. I felt sick because of the smell.' What was Malone talking about?
5. What happened to the explorers' camp?

7

1. The second night in the Lost World something woke the explorers. What did they hear? What did they see? What did Lord Roxton do?
2. What was strange about the dead iguanodon?
3. Why did Malone climb a tree?
4. While he was climbing the tree Malone had a shock. What did he see?
5. What did Malone see when he reached the top of the tree?
6. What promise did Challenger make?

8

1. Malone went for a walk. What frightened him?
2. What did Malone see on the other side of the lake?
3. Why did Malone fall into the dinosaur trap?

4 What did Malone find when he got back to the camp?
5 Who did Malone go and speak to?

9

1 Roxton told Malone what had happened in the camp. What had happened?
2 Where did Malone and Roxton go? What did they see?
3 How was Summerlee saved from the Ape-People?
4 Who followed the explorers back to their camp?

10

1 What happened to Malone on the way to the Indians' caves?
2 What did the explorers find out about the young Indian?
3 How were the explorers going to help the Indians?
4 What did the explorers find out about the iguanodons?
5 Who won the battle on the plateau?

11

1 Why were the Indians safe in their caves?
2 One day Malone saw something strange at the pterodactyl pit. What was it?
3 Who helped the explorers leave the Lost World? How did he help them?
4 How did the explorers get out of the Lost World?

12

1 What did Professor Summerlee tell the audience in the Zoological Institute?
2 What did Dr Illingworth ask Professor Challenger to do?
3 What had Professor Challenger brought from the Lost World? What did it do?
4 Why did people now believe in the Lost World?

Heinemann English Language Teaching
A division of Reed Educational and Professional Publishing Limited
Halley Court, Jordan Hill, Oxford OX2 8EJ

OXFORD MADRID FLORENCE ATHENS PRAGUE
SÃO PAULO MEXICO CITY CHICAGO PORTSMOUTH (NH)
TOKYO SINGAPORE KUALA LUMPUR MELBOURNE
AUCKLAND JOHANNESBURG IBADAN GABORONE

SBN 0 435 27318 3

This retold version for Heinemann Guided Readers
Text © Anne Collins 1995
Design and illustration © Heinemann Publishers (Oxford) Ltd 1995
First published 1995

All rights reserved; no part of this publication may be
reproduced, stored in a retrieval system, transmitted in any
form, or by any means, electronic, mechanical, photocopying,
recording, or otherwise, without the prior written permission of
the publishers.

Illustrated by Kathy Stephen
Typography by Adrian Hodgkins
Designed by Sue Vaudin
Cover by Graham Humphreys and Marketplace Design
Set in 11.5/14.5 Goudy
Printed and bound in Malta